THE AMAZING THE INCREDIBLE SUPER DOG

by Crosby Bonsall

HarperCollins*Publishers*

For Nina w.w.

with love

The Amazing The Incredible Super Dog
Copyright © 1986 by Crosby Bonsall
Printed in the U.S.A. All rights reserved.
10 9 8 7 6 5 4 3

Library of Congress Cataloging-in-Publication Data
Bonsall, Crosby Newell, date
  The amazing the incredible super dog.

  Summary: A little girl brags to her cat about the
tricks she teaches her dog, unaware that her cat can do
them all.
  [1. Dogs—Fiction. 2. Cats—Fiction] I. Title.
PZ7.B64265Am 1986   [E]   85-45811
ISBN 0-06-020590-3
ISBN 0-06-020591-1 (lib. bdg.)

THE AMAZING
THE INCREDIBLE
SUPER DOG

Want to meet my puppy?

Her name is Super Dog.

She can do a hundred tricks

fast as anything.

My cat Willy is jealous.

I love him a lot,

but cats can't do tricks.

or her very first trick
Super Dog will stand
on her back legs.

Let's go, Super Dog!

ow stand on your front legs.

THE MAZIN
TH INCREDIBL
SUPER DOG

ext, show them how you beg,
Super Dog.

And now, the back flip.

Whooeee!

ou better rest, Super Dog.

ow, let's do a split.

This is a great show, Super Dog!

THE

T IN REDI

UPE DOG

uper Dog will now stand on her head.

ext, jump through this hoop.

ome on, Super Dog.

THE TIRED DOG

Ahhhhh, Super Dog!
You've saved the best trick
for last.

Isn't she amazing?

Isn't she incredible?

Didn't I tell you?

Super Dog is playing dead!

Oh Willy,

if you could only do tricks,

you could be like Super Dog!